My Big
FANTASTIC
Family

For Clare and her big fantastic family!
—A. G. and C. G.

For families of all shapes and sizes.
—A. P.

First published 2021 by Nosy Crow Ltd.
Wheat Wharf, 27a Shad Thames, London, SE1 2XZ, UK

This edition published 2023 by Nosy Crow Inc.
Nosy Crow Inc. 145 Lincoln Road, Lincoln, MA 01773, USA

www.nosycrow.com

ISBN 979-8-88777-030-7

Nosy Crow and its logos are trademarks of Nosy Crow Ltd.
Used under license.

Text © Adam and Charlotte Guillain 2021
Illustrations © Ali Pye 2021

Library of Congress Catalog Card Number pending.

Printed in China
Papers used by Nosy Crow are made from wood grown in sustainable forests.
10 9 8 7 6 5 4 3 2 1

Written by Adam & Charlotte Guillain

My Big FANTASTIC Family

Illustrated by Ali Pye

Hello! My name is Lily-May.
I live with Mom, not Dad.

A lot of things have had to change,
and sometimes I feel sad.

When Mom and Dad first told me
Dad was going to move away,
I hugged Blue Bear and shouted, "No!"
I wanted Dad to stay.

I felt all upside-down inside,
but they both hugged me tight.

"It's **not** your fault," they said to me,
"It's going to be alright."

So Dad drives down on Sundays now,
and we go out to play.
I **always** take Blue Bear with me
to share our special day.

We **love** to do exciting things,
like riding super fast.
We race our bikes downhill,
and people gasp as we zoom past!

I play more with just Mom now, too.
We read books all the time.

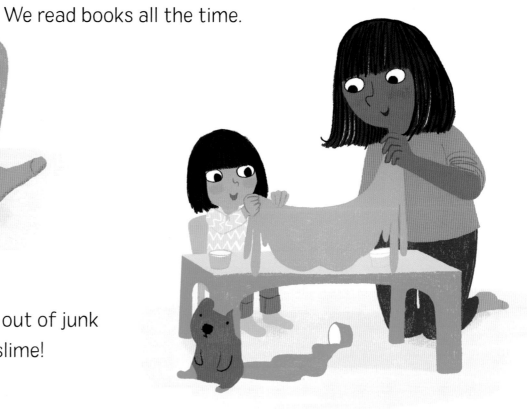

We make more models out of junk
and play with squidgy slime!

There's more time to make stories up—
more stories mean more fun!

And now my mom's with Peter—
well, there's more of . . .
everyone!

I used to just have Granny—
now there's Gramps and Grandma G.
That's Peter's mom and dad,
they're **great** at playing games with me.

There's Ben now, and there's Theo, too—
they're Peter's older boys.
They come to stay on Saturdays,
and now we have more . . . noise!

But when Mom started working late,
the first time Peter cooked,
I didn't like his spicy sauce
or how the noodles looked.

I wanted Dad to cook for me
the way that I like best . . .

I scrunched my eyes up tight
and felt a thumping in my chest.

I tried to **wish** things back
to when they didn't feel mixed up.

Then Peter made hot chocolate for me
in my special cup.

We read some bedtime stories,
then we sang a funny song.

When Mom came home,
she **hugged** me,
and she laughed and sang along!

Next day, I went to stay with Dad.
I knew it would be great.

My bag was stuffed with toys and books.
I really couldn't wait!

And when at last Mom dropped me off,
Dad suddenly appeared.
"I've got a **big surprise**," he said . . .

"Oh, wow! A cat!"
I cheered.

Dad showed me how to feed her,

and she found a place to hide.

I made a secret fort with Dad
and **snuggled** up inside.

But later on, when bedtime came,
I brushed my teeth and hair,

then had a really awful thought,
and asked Dad,

"Where's Blue Bear?"

We looked under the covers,
and my heart began to pound.

We ran around, searched
high and low . . .

. . . Blue Bear could **not** be found!

So Dad gave me a hug, and then
we called Mom on the phone . . .

"I've just tucked Blue Bear in," she said.
"Don't cry—he's not alone."

The next day, when Dad drove me back,
he had a chat with Mom.
We planned my birthday party
and invited . . . everyone!

So me and Mom picked party games,
while Peter baked some cakes.
Then Ben and Theo added sprinkles,
and some chocolate flakes!

Then when **at last** the big day came,
I waited by the door.
I thought about how things have changed . . .

... and how there's so much more!

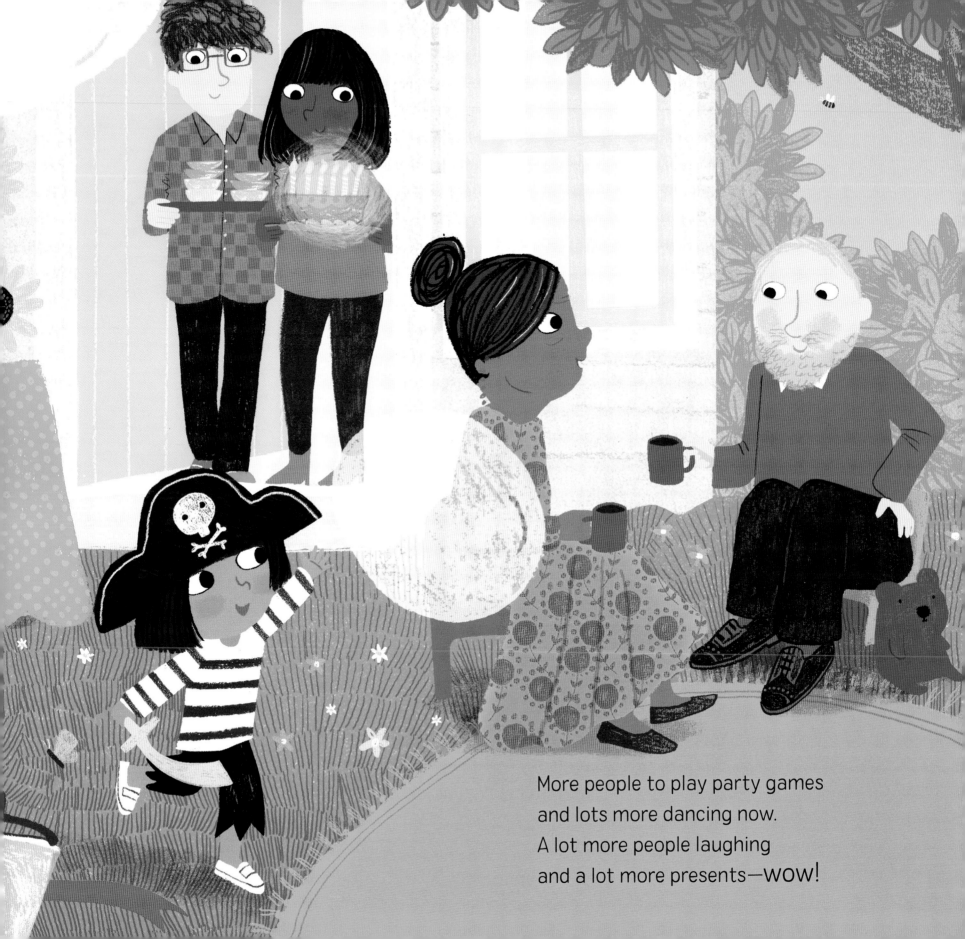

More people to play party games
and lots more dancing now.
A lot more people laughing
and a lot more presents—WOW!

I say goodbye more often now,
but when it's time to go,
I know goodbye will only last
until our next hello.

I've got more places I belong.
"Where's home?" my friends ask me.

It's anywhere I'm with
my **big** fantastic family.